AF433827

I SHOULD HAVE WORN A CURTAIN

A Novella

SAMYRA ALEXANDER

OTHER TITLES BY SAMYRA ALEXANDER

Road to Malevolence: A Novel

I SHOULD HAVE WORN A CURTAIN SERIES

I Should Have Worn A Curtain: A Novella
I Should Have Worn A Curtain 2: A Novella

CONTENTS

CHAPTER 1

I woke up five minutes ago, and it's already 1:30 pm. Luckily, it's my day off from the nursing home. I work there as an administrative assistant.

I'm sitting on the storage bench at the foot of my bed, my face buried in my hands, still feeling stuffed from yesterday's binge. I ate a dozen donuts and an extra-large pizza. My intentions were pure. The goal was to reward myself with one donut for sticking to my diet. After eating my treat, I instantly craved more and found myself back at the bakery. Then, coming out of the bakery, I got a craving for pizza when I spotted the pizza joint.

I feel awful that I couldn't stop eating, and now I'm paying for my indulgence with nausea and a massive headache. It feels like I've gained ten pounds overnight, probably putting me over three hundred pounds. Ugh.

This isn't a positive start to my day.

After I binged, I didn't force myself to throw up. I never do that because I hate vomiting, and I read somewhere it negatively affects the body. Some time ago, I typed in my symptoms online to determine what's wrong with me, and, according to Google, I have an eating disorder. I can't bring myself to say it, though. Not even to myself because of something I learned from Nana. Rest in peace, Nana.

She said anyone believing in God who named and claimed illness lacked faith that Jesus' sacrifice on the cross had healed every past, present, and future disease. Nana had hypertension, but she'd never put it that way. Instead, she would declare that the doctors said she had hypertension, but she was already healed by Jesus' stripes. I'm not religious like she was, but her words stuck with me.

Admitting I binge differs from saying, "I'm Shaena, and I'm bulimic." Accepting that label would define me, but that's not who I am.

I'll overcome my problem with diet and exercise.

I feel the need to go for a walk to make up for what I did last night. Calories don't burn themselves after all. I lift my head from my hands and the room spins, a wave of nausea hitting me. I lay my head against my palms again and get some relief, but it's immediately shattered by the sound of my neighbor's howls of laughter. She's so loud I can clearly imagine her bent over and holding her stomach. Since there's no audible response, I assume she's on the phone. She blithely tells the other person on the line that she brought a coworker home last night and the sex was mediocre. Apparently, he had left out foreplay.

I'm not intentionally eavesdropping, the walls are thin and that neighbor is always hollering about something. I blame the noise on my overpriced building that hasn't seen a remodel since the 1980s.

She shrieks with laughter again, and my body jerks, making me kick the five-pound weight next to my foot. I wince and grasp my toes in my hands, looking to the ceiling. Can this day get any worse?

The silk bedsheet wrapped around my body falls, forcing me to look at my fat rolls and cellulite. I yank the sheet back up. Why is it so much easier to put on weight than to lose it? I've never woken up after a day of dieting and exercising with noticeable fat loss.

Life is unfair. I'll probably die fat and alone.

My cell phone rings, so I reach for it. It's my father. I stare at the screen blankly. I don't feel up for talking. When the call goes to voicemail, I'm conflicted because I'd like to wish him a happy Sunday, but then Mother will get on the phone and make me sicker than I already am. I don't even care to talk to her on a good day.

A few moments later, a voicemail comes through.

"Hey, Baby Girl. I'm putting some meat on the grill. Stop by if you can. Haven't seen you in a while. Here's your mother."

The sound of the phone being handed off to my mother crackles through my phone speaker.

"Shaena, why does your father have to bribe you with food to come and see your parents? Are you still exercising? You have got to get that weight off. There's a new gym near the house offering a free trial. You should check it out with me. You stay in that apartment too much. All you do is go to work and come home. You're too young to live like that. Talk soon."

That's why I didn't answer. How does Dad put up with her? If I needed her help, I'd ask. After all these years, she hasn't learned that my weight isn't her concern.

Is it too late to be adopted by another mother?

I stare at the framed affirmations hanging on my wall to distract myself from my weight.

"You're a conqueror"

"Believe in yourself"

"You are 100% victorious"

Yes, I'm all of those things. I should push past my exhaustion and move, but I don't want to tip over and fall off the bench. The last thing I need is to have the downstairs neighbor rushing to my door trying to figure out what caused the sudden loud noise.

People my size are constantly afraid of falling. There's nothing more embarrassing than a big person crashing to the ground and struggling to get up. I wouldn't need help getting up, but it would take some time, and with my luck, an idiot with a camera would capture my humiliation. People are just that cruel.

My eyes widen as I feel my stomach rumble. I quickly get up and rush for the bathroom, dodging the pillow I left on the floor. Why is it when I'm binging I never consider how I'll feel afterward? Diarrhea is no joke.

As I'm drying my hands, I side-eye my bathroom scale against the wall. I inch toward it because I'm a glutton for punishment. Stepping on the scale, I look down and recoil.

I've gained eight pounds.

That can't be right, so I get off and try again. A feeling of dread fills me as I reach for the tape measure on the shelf and wrap it around my waist. I gained two inches around my stomach. How will I fit into my jeans? They fit snug before today.

I grab two laxatives from the medicine cabinet and quickly swallow them, hoping the pills will prevent any more weight gain. How did I become such a mess? I'm thirty-one, and I've been binge eating since I was a teenager. After each episode, I lie and say that I'll never do it again, but I always go back to what I do best—shoveling food down my throat.

My eyes roam around the bedroom, taking in the mess I made last night. The fitted sheet is balled up in the center of the bed, and I'm currently wearing the top sheet. The clothes I binged in last night lie discarded on the floor. Sometime during the night I tossed them because it was another scorcher in Los Angeles.

As I make my bed, the smell of hickory seeps through the walls, causing me to gag. I head to the blinds and open them to discover the source of the gut-churning scent. Someone is flipping burgers in the courtyard. The food looks good, but burgers aren't a part of my diet. I can get back on track tomorrow. From now on, there'll be no more cheating, and I'll stay focused.

I grab a pair of ripped blue jeans from my walk-in closet and almost pass out sliding them up my thighs. These *have* to be jeans without spandex. Looking at the tag, I'm horrified because these are the ones with five percent spandex. I sigh. Must it be this difficult to stuff my apple-shaped body into these size twenty-two jeans?

Perhaps I could wear a curtain instead. It would be roomier than my jeans. It's no different from dressing in a toga for a costume party. Sure, I'd get some stares, but never mind what people think. I can adorn it with pink bows and a wide gold belt. I'd wear my favorite gold earrings and put my locs in a bun. My pink heels would look nice with my curtain, but black pumps would be more suitable because people say black makes one look slimmer. A woman should be able to wear a curtain fashionably when clothes turn into her worst enemy.

I like to imagine how a conversation with my jeans would go. "Hey, jeans, I thought you and I were supposed to love one another. You know, until death do us part. What have I done for you to treat me so badly?"

"Shaena, stop shoving your big bottom into me," my jeans would say. "You accuse me, but now it's my turn to hold court with you. You annihilated my inner and outer thigh seams. You pull and tug at me so mercilessly, and if that's not inhumane enough, you nearly tore off my button and left it hanging on by a thread. Don't even get me started about my zipper. The damage is unthinkable. It used to zip perfectly, and now it's off-track from the pressure of your man hands."

I lay on my bed, still wrestling with my jeans to pull them up. I'm the master of my jeans. If I say jeans are on, they're on. Even if they're too small, I'm still in control.

I haven't always been at war with my jeans. There was a time when I was thirty pounds lighter and my jeans were happy. How I miss those days. It seemed as if the sun shone brighter, the moon smiled at me, and the crickets leapt to greet me when I opened my front door. But now, my jeans are punishing me. I imagine one day I'll abandon pants in favor of skirts because they're more forgiving, and all of my jeans will applaud, saying, "At last, we're free!"

My T-shirt is misbehaving now, too. It used to fit, but now it clings to my skin and shows my back rolls.

I've had it with my clothes. I can't go on like this.

CHAPTER 2

Grabbing my phone from the nightstand, I call Over-eaters Anonymous, otherwise simply known as OA. After last week's binge, I researched OA and saved the number. I hope OA will teach me how to stop binging so I can finally lose weight, but I don't have to tell them that's why I'm doing the program. I'll lie and say I'm just an overeater, but they don't need to know about the binging or the laxatives. I don't like the idea of opening up to strangers, but I have to at least try a little.

A woman picks up and introduces herself as Ava. "You did the right thing by reaching out," she says. "The first call is the hardest."

Her voice is soothing, but I'm immediately suspicious of how freely she revealed her name. So much for confidentiality. "You don't have to give your name if you don't want to," Ava continues. "I'm a sponsor at OA. How can I help?"

"I'm Shaena," I say my name out of habit, immediately regretting it. I'm supposed to be anonymous. "I might not say my name at OA to protect my privacy," I add hastily. I need her to know that so she doesn't blurt my name out if we attend the same group.

"You don't have to share anything you're uncomfortable with," she assures me.

I exhale in relief. "I'm calling because I overeat sometimes and I need help to lose weight. Yesterday, I had three donuts and ate a small pizza. How do I join?"

"I can relate to feeling out of control with food," Ava tells me. "For years, I binged and made myself sick. You wouldn't believe the money I spent on food. My addiction nearly ended my marriage. I hear you want to lose weight, but our focus is to stop compulsive eating. We're not a diet group."

Why participate in a support group if I won't get skinny and sexy? I'll glean whatever knowledge I learn from the group and apply it to weight loss. No one has to know my true agenda, but I am glad she can relate to what I'm going through.

"That's fine. Being a part of a like-minded support group community is what's most important to me." I can't stop lying.

"I like the sound of that. Some members lose weight because of managing their eating habits. How did you hear about us?" Ava asks.

"I watched online videos and visited the website. People had good things to say about OA," I respond.

"Thanks for considering us. Our website has our locations, dates, and times. I'm at the West LA location. I'd like to have you with us, but I understand if it's out of your way."

"Thanks. I'll check it out," I reply, hoping I don't have to drive too far and sit in traffic to get to a meeting. "What can I expect at a meeting?"

"Sure. Our meetings resemble Alcoholic Anonymous. We adhere to OA's 12 Steps. We're anonymous. It's a group setting where people share their wins and challenges, and we have sponsors to assist members on their journey. There's no fee." After a short pause, she adds, "I know that's a lot to take in."

"It is, but I appreciate knowing what I'm getting into. I have no more questions. Thanks for your time," I say.

"Call if you think of more questions, and best of luck," says Ava.

Once I hang up, I search through OA's website and see that there's a meeting nearby this afternoon. This day is looking up. How many calories will I burn if I walk? Two hundred maybe. Some people maintain mental agility with crossword puzzles, but calorie counting is what keeps me sharp. If I'm going to be a part of OA, I have to do it today, or else I'll change my mind. I have a habit of getting excited about new diets and then losing interest. It only took three Weight Watchers meetings for me to dump the calculator in my closet, never to be seen again. I won't let myself get weary of OA. I need to make a change.

In the kitchen, I flick on the light and grab a water bottle and snack. My motto is to never leave home without food. I glance at the coffee pot, and now I want coffee, creamer, and several packs of sugar, but sugar is off-limits now. At one time, tasting something sweet would make me want more, but that was the old me. I turn off the light and glance at the empty pizza box and donut container shoved in the trash. I shake my head, walking past it to the front door. I'm too tired to clean. My jeans dig into my stomach, so I pull them down under my belly. Taking a deep breath, I head out the door and take my first step towards OA.

After taking a few steps down the sidewalk, I put in my earbuds. I have to move out of the way because people in workout clothes are running toward me, sweating and huffing. They must go to the gym up the street. I could never join that gym because whenever I walk past, I'm intimidated by the fit people. They obviously know what they're doing. Look at them and look at me. If I looked as good as them, I'd never work out. Maybe that's my problem: I don't think like thin people.

Ahead of me is the finest man I've seen all week. I stare, although I don't want to for obvious reasons. He catches me watching him and stops, giving me a pleasant smile. I'm astounded at the gesture because I've walked this block for years, and gym rats never approach me. He's wearing white compression tights under yellow shorts and a yellow and black tank top. His biceps are something to marvel at as beads of sweat drip down them.

I smile and look up at his tanned skin and brown eyes while he's rubbing his hand across a freshly cut fade. "I'm Mike. I just moved here from back East. I'm a personal trainer at a place called CrossFit. What's your name?"

"I'm Shaena. Welcome to LA and congrats on the job. What's it like working at the gym?" I hope he doesn't notice I'm blushing. Do black people blush? I must Google that later.

"Thanks for the welcome." He pauses, focusing on the ground. "It's been a challenge building up my clientele because I'm new, but I'm working on it." He waves a hand dismissively. "But you don't want to hear me ramble about that. How are you? Are you single?"

"I don't have a man." I'm twisting with my sweating hands in my pocket.

Is he about to ask me out?

A personal trainer has never asked about my relationship status.

What's going on here?

He winks. "Good, because I'm single too. I like big, beautiful women, as you all have the most potential."

I recoil slightly. Is he trying to offend me? If he wants me to sign up for his class, he's going about it all wrong.

He rubs his hand down my arm. I glare at him and step back, and his hand falls away. Why did he think he could say that with impunity? Noticing my hesitation, he laughs to fill the awkward space. "I can see what I said upset you. I mean no harm, so don't cut me." He gestures to himself. "I'm a giver, and all I want to do is help everyone live a long, healthy life."

Is he toxic?

I should walk off, but he intrigues me. "Were you trying to be disrespectful?" I ask, cocking my head to the side.

"I'm blunt. It's a good and bad quality." He grins. "I'd never try to hurt anyone. You don't know me, but you can if you'd like. Let me show you I'm one of the few good men left. "He smiles in the way all confident men do when they know a woman finds them captivating.

"I'm not in a hurry." Glancing at my cell phone, it shows I have plenty of time to get to OA. Warming up to Mike, I move closer. If he asks me directly, I'll buy a gym membership and attend every day he's there.

He called himself blunt? Well, I'll give him the benefit of the doubt because he's probably upfront with everyone.

Of course, I want to get to know him. He's into health, and I want to be healthy.

Will he ask me out?

"Before we go any further, let me test your knowledge." He folds his arms. "Which is better: Whole Foods or Trader Joe's?"

"Easy. Whole Foods," I say confidently, knowing there could only be one answer. What does he mean by "before we go any further?" Is he about to give me a gift card if I join the gym? Does CrossFit have a new marketing technique?

He clicks his tongue disapprovingly. "I have much to teach you. Trader Joe's is the best because they have better quality multivitamins, fish oil tablets, and protein powder." He nods, satisfied that his response seems to end the debate.

"Get out of here," I say. "Whole Foods has a wider variety of supplements, and they set the standard for healthy eating." I laugh to make him think this conversation is funny.

He pulls a business card out of his pocket and looks at it. I knew it. He's about to offer me his services. I'm the biggest person on both sides of the street. It's obvious I could benefit from his help. Dumb me for thinking he wanted anything more.

Rather than hand me the card, he hands it to a man who comes from behind and passes me.

"Hey," Mike says to the man. "I'm Mike, and I work as a trainer at CrossFit up the street. Call me if you need a trainer or have nutrition questions. I'm offering a promotional package this week."

"Thanks, bro. I'll be in touch." The man pockets the card and heads off.

Mike turns to me, smiling, and continues where he left off, launching into a lengthy monologue about supplements and superfoods. I nod along and try to look interested, but I'm already tired of this conversation. I shop at Whole Foods and Trader Joe's occasionally, but what's a superfood?

"You've convinced me, you're a clever genius." I force a smile, not wanting to appear sarcastic, although I'm absolutely being sarcastic. My mind is telling me to walk away. There's no depth. My lonely heart is hoping Mike the health nut will reveal more of a personality. Seeming to notice my disinterest, his voice softens.

"You looked lost when I was talking about ancient grains. Let me take you out one day and I'll show you. You can eat well and have food that tastes great. Let me get your number."

It can't be true.

He asked me out.

But why?

The women I assumed were from his gym who ran past me earlier look nothing like me. He's likely their trainer and could have any of them. Is he up to something malevolent? Maybe he's hoping I'll pay his bills and take care of him, but I've never been that desperate and never will be.

I flash him an incredulous look as we exchange numbers. Does he chop up fat women and eat them to maintain his good looks?

"I'll text you so you can lock in my number." He licks his lips and walks off.

Still dazed from what just happened, I head to my first OA meeting. Did I make the right decision by giving him my number? No, I'm being negative again. There's more to him than whole grains, I know it.

What will I wear? Now that's more positive thinking.

Where will he take me? I'll be nervous about eating in front of him, but he asked me out knowing I'm plus size. Hopefully, if everything works out, I'll show him some of my favorite places around the city.

CHAPTER 3

Standing outside the one-story recreation center where the OA group meets, I watch as people walk in and out. Some smile when they see me, and I force a strained grin. I don't see anyone as big as me. I'm surprised at all the normal-sized and super-thin people. This must be the wrong address.

I check Google Maps, and, unfortunately, I'm at the right place. Closing my eyes and exhaling, I try to channel a calmness I don't know if I have, telling myself that if I'm going to do this, I need to go inside. The meeting starts soon.

I follow an OA sign that leads me to a room with fifteen others—it's a mix of women and men, but mostly women. I'm unhappy about being the biggest one in the room, but I'll try not to focus on that. Healthy me will do whatever is necessary to get control of my eating.

There's a podium upfront and I stare at it, knowing I might never stand behind it. All I need is minimal encouragement, so there's no need to tell the room about every embarrassing eating experience I've had.

I grab a seat in the empty back row, and everyone in the row ahead turns and smiles. I smile back weakly, but I hope no one comes to chat. I can't divulge that I'm here to lose weight. My eyes keep frantically glancing at the door. No one I know had better show up here.

A woman soon opens the group by reciting the serenity prayer. She's wearing a sundress, and it's obvious she goes to the gym.

Did I overlook something in the online description? Everyone here is supposed to be overweight.

I smile because the voice belongs to Ava, the person I spoke to when I called. What's her story?

"Veterans of the group, we have new faces! Give our guests a round of applause for taking a big first step." A bout of clapping follows, and after it dies down, Ava continues. "I'm one of the sponsors here, so please see me after the group if you have questions. I can introduce you to the other sponsors. Sponsors, wave your hands." I don't have to look around the room. I know who I want as my sponsor.

"I think everyone can agree that we've all tried to heal ourselves but to no avail," says Ava, her eyes passing over the group. "At OA, we understand the need for a higher power and a community to help manage food addictions."

Her words surprise me. I'm struggling, but I didn't know I need God's intervention. However, I *have* tried to deal with this problem on my own and failed miserably. Food is just so darn good—better than a friend—after a stressful day.

"I came to OA after years of battling bulimia," Ava says to us, looking at everyone in the crowd as she speaks. "I tried weight loss clinics and therapists, but nothing worked until I came here and got an accountability partner. My sponsor has no problem telling me when I'm slipping back into old habits." She blows a kiss to a man in the front row who I assume is her sponsor.

I begin to fiddle with the hem of my shirt. Am I ready for a sponsor?

"I developed an eating disorder after I quit my job to become a full-time mom," Ava continues. "I gave my husband and daughter my all and stopped connecting with friends and extended family. I got depressed because I had no interests other than waiting for my husband to get home so he could hear about my day." She shrugs. "I gravitated towards food because I thought it was safer than alcohol. Both of my parents are alcoholics, and I swore I'd never go down that path, but I became an addict all right: a food addict. Dieting turned into an extreme diet and exercise routine, and later I binged and purged to avoid getting bigger."

The audience sits in silence as they listen, soaking in her story. Somberly, she continues, "I've been where you are, so I can help guide you, but you have to do the work. The 12 Steps can help you stop disordered eating just as it did for me. I got my life on track by reconnecting with loved ones and developing hobbies." She smiles at us. "Keep coming to meetings and participate when you're ready. One day, you too could be a sponsor."

She walks back to her seat as we all clap for her. A man came in while Ava was speaking and sat a seat over from me. He's wearing a dark suit jacket that refuses to conceal his stomach. After a moment, he leans over to me and whispers, "I've never seen you. Welcome." He extends his hand, we shake, then he points to Ava. "That woman knows her stuff. She's been sponsoring me for a year now."

"Thanks." I glance down nervously at his jacket button that may pop off with any sudden move. "She seems nice." I face the front as the facilitator invites others to share.

I now have confirmation that Ava is who I need by my side. She's skinny, but she seems genuine. I'm a little concerned, though, that the man next to me has been with Ava a year and is still fat, but I'm being harsh. He could've been fatter a year ago.

A pudgy Latina steps to the podium and sets her purse on the table nearby. "I met my goal this week! I didn't eat my daughter's snacks," she says, beaming. "I took your guys' suggestions and bought snacks of my own like fruit with Tajin, Chamoy, and lime juice. My daughter surprised me because she's been listening to me more. I asked what had changed, and she said I stopped eating her Takis and Gansitos." She shrugs and giggles. We all chuckle with her.

How well does she know this group of people to admit she stole her daughter's snacks?

"If I had known she'd stop being a little terror, I would've left her chips alone sooner," says the Latina. "I'm still tempted, but self-control feels good, and I enjoy peace with my daughter." She heads to her seat when she's done as we give her applause.

At the end of the group session, I don't feel bad about not participating and sharing my story. It's my first day after all. I rise from my seat and join others in line to speak to Ava. She talks with her hands and touches everyone she greets.

What will she think about being my sponsor?

Now, face to face with Ava, I say, "We spoke on the phone earlier. I'm Shaena. Can we talk privately?" People are lingering a few feet away, and I can do without an audience. She nods and I follow her as she leads me to the back row.

"I'm so happy you showed," says Ava, light dancing behind her eyes. "What would you like to talk about?"

I uneasily twist my locs between my shaking fingers.

How much will she get into my business?

Am I ready to commit to whatever her expectations are?

I clear my throat before saying, "I want you to be my sponsor. I'm ready for a change and think you'll be able to help."

I got it out. I'm seldom bold, but after my last binge, I'm desperate for a change.

Her eyes soften and she puts her hands over her heart. "I'm flattered you selected me as your sponsor. Are you sure you don't want to come to more meetings and get to know the other sponsors?"

Instantly, I shake my head no.

"I encourage everyone I sponsor to keep a food diary," continues Ava. "That way, you and I will know what you're eating and how you feel after each meal. It's tedious, but it works." She stands. "Be right back." She rushes to a table behind us and grabs a few pamphlets and a book, passing them over to me as she sits down. "It's a lot to read but take your time. It explains our philosophy and the food diary. Take my number and call if you have questions."

We exchange numbers all the while I'm a little giddy. I'm looking forward to working with her. "I can't wait to learn more about the program. Keeping a journal won't be a problem."

"What type of work do you do?" Ava asks, crossing her legs.

I frown slightly, not sure how knowing that will help me lose weight. "I've worked as an administrative assistant at a nursing home since I graduated from high school."

"How do you like it?"

I hunch my shoulders, uncomfortable with the subject. "It's a job, but I don't want to retire there." I don't want to tell her I'm too comfortable to leave even though I'd prefer doing something creative.

"I get it," Ava says. "Is it stressful?"

I look to the floor. "Not at all."

More people are walking out, and I assume Ava will get up to leave, but she says, "Is it alright if we discuss your upbringing? I often find food issues begin in childhood." She looks away from me for a second to wave goodbye to a member. Returning to me, she continues, "You don't have to share more than you are comfortable with. Is that okay with you?"

I'm shifting in my seat. "Is that really necessary? Will I get better if I talk about my past?" That was a loaded question asking about my childhood. She could've at least pulled out a couch and let me lay down.

Ava nods. "It's helpful to explore one's history to learn about overeating triggers. Although, it might take us getting to know one another more before we identify your triggers. You're uncomfortable opening up to a stranger. That's natural." She smiles. "I'll sponsor you."

I can't help but smile back. Her eyes are trustworthy, and she doesn't look prone to gossip. Since she thinks it'll help, I'll do it. If I'm going to lose weight, I have to step outside my comfort zone. I didn't think it would be this far outside, but I will do it.

After a deep breath, I say, "I'm an only child, raised by both my dad and my mother until I was twelve. Mother disappeared the night before my thirteenth birthday."

"I'm sorry," Ava says, resting her hand on top of mine.

Her touch is soothing, motivating me to continue. "Don't be sorry," I say more forcefully than I mean to. "Aliens didn't abduct her. No one kidnapped her and forced her into human trafficking. She left willingly. As a goodbye, she left a note under my bedroom door saying she loved me, and her leaving wasn't because of me." An empty and seemingly endless pause follows before I pick up again. "My parents argued, but I didn't know it was that bad. I gained weight not long after she left. Anytime I felt sad or angry, I ate and felt better."

Talking about my past resurfaces memories I'd like to forget. I don't tell Ava I must've read Mother's letter every day for an entire year. She left me with so many questions. Couldn't she have run away the day after my birthday? Why didn't she say goodbye in person? Why not take me with her?

What kind of woman abandons her family?

"What you experienced would be enough to make anyone stressed. People cope in different ways," says Ava, her tone soft. "What happened after she left? Did she call?"

Why didn't Mother want me? Had she loved me and Dad, she would've stayed.

"There were times I heard my dad crying himself to sleep. He never wanted to discuss her leaving. He'd only say Mother loved me and wanted the best for me. He was fine, and her leaving had nothing to do with me." I throw my hands up in frustration because, of course, as a child, I blamed myself for her leaving. What child doesn't question if they're responsible for their parents' divorce or separation? "Mother never called, visited, or wrote."

Ava rubbed the back of my hand reassuringly. "That's a lot for a young girl to go through. You said don't be sorry, but I am sorry you went through that. Your mother left without a face-to-face goodbye. Why do you refer to your mother as 'Mother'?"

A knot forms in my stomach at the mention of her, and I choose my words carefully. I want to condemn her for leaving, but I don't want to despise her more than I already do. "Mother is a formal word, and it high-lights her less-than motherly ways."

Will any good come of talking about my family?

Ava nods. "I see. How did your life change after she left?"

She's not letting up. How much do I want her to know?

Pushing back against my discomfort, I answer. "My dad took on more hours at work to supplement mother's income. Fortunately, my mother's sister, Patricia, began coming to the house to help. I took over a lot of the cooking and cleaning to help Dad."

"Sounds like you had a good support system. Teen years are when a girl really needs her mother," says Ava, shaking her head again. "I couldn't imagine not having mine. The fact you got through those years without yours tells me you're resilient. Feeling abandoned can make one overly dependent on food for comfort."

I fight a smile. No one has ever called me resilient, and I appreciate it. I didn't feel resilient when I woke up this morning, but here I am now, taking the first step towards recovery.

I study Ava warily. She's easy to talk to, but I'm still hesitant. Will Ava think badly of me if I tell her how I truly feel about Mother? People are fickle and quick to judge, but perhaps she's right about why I overeat.

If Mother hadn't left me, would my life have turned out differently?

Ava looks down at her phone and then smiles back up at me apologetically. "I have to get going, but I'll be in touch. I'll text you some positive affirmations, and you can send me some if you have any good ones. Even sponsors need encouragement." We stand and she gingerly touches my arm. "Thanks for opening up. I'm hoping that you'll continue to open up gradually so I'll know how best to work with you. We'll talk later."

I thank her for listening, and I'm relieved as we walk to the exit. If we'd gone any longer, I'd need a dessert to stop feeling awful. I like her, so I'll definitely be back.

After we leave the building and part ways, I take a two-hour walk to burn yesterday's calories and then head home to flop onto my sofa in a tired heap.

CHAPTER 4

I'm debating if I should text Mike, but I don't want to appear desperate. It's been days, and he hasn't texted. I probably should delete his number. Shaking my head, I convince myself that I'm better off without him. He seems the type of guy that would have me at the gym lifting tires and rope climbing, and I'm not about that life.

I open Ava's messages to read the affirmations she sent me. I don't believe them, especially today's one: "I love and accept my body as it is." The words pass through me like a hollow echo. I haven't deleted them in the hopes that one day they might resonate with me.

I set down my phone and grab the OA materials from the table in front of me to read the 12 Steps of Over-eaters Anonymous.

1. We admitted we were powerless over food—that our lives had become unmanageable.

2. Came to believe that a power greater than ourselves could restore us to sanity.

3. Made a decision to turn our will and our lives over to the care of God as we understood Him.

4. Made a searching and fearless moral inventory of ourselves.

5. Admitted to God, to ourselves, and to another human being the exact nature of our wrongs.

6. Were entirely ready to have God remove all these defects of character.

7. Humbly asked Him to remove our shortcomings.

8. Made a list of all persons we had harmed, and became willing to make amends to them all.

9. Made direct amends to such people wherever possible, except when to do so would injure them or others.

10. Continued to take personal inventory and when we were wrong, promptly admitted it.

11. Sought through prayer and meditation to improve our conscious contact with God as we understood Him, praying only for knowledge of His will for us and the power to carry that out.

12. Having had a spiritual awakening as the result of these Steps, we tried to carry this message to compulsive overeaters and to practice these principles in all our affairs.

Sheesh. That's a lot to comprehend at once.

There's a lot about God. Can He help? Will he send Gabriel or Michael to assist? Do the angels not have more pressing matters to tend to, or would they want me to keep trying my best?

Step 1 is true. Out of control eating is why I have this pamphlet in my hands. I'll keep coming to meetings to learn how people apply the steps in their daily lives. It's unclear if I do one step at a time or do them all at once, but I won't burden myself because I have time to learn about the steps.

My phone chimes and I pick it up.

"Hey, beautiful. Want to go get something to eat tomorrow?"

I stare at the text from Mike, wide-eyed.

He called me beautiful?

Why has it taken Mike so long to text?

I shake off the doubts in my mind, telling myself that he's probably just busy. At any rate, he'll have to wait on a response because I don't want to seem overeager. And I'm hungry.

In the kitchen, I make dinner of grilled fish, salad, and mixed vegetables with no fat. I jot down my food in the journal I bought at Ava's suggestion. It's annoying to track meals, but if that's what it takes to be thin,

I'm all in. I'm eating right and haven't binged since the day before joining OA.

Once I'm done washing dishes, I text Mike.

"Hey! Surprise me. Can't wait."

A moment later, the phone buzzes again.

"I got you. I'll text the details. Stay blessed."

I feel my cheeks heat up a bit. He's wishing blessings on me, that's considerate. I can't wait to see him, but I hope he talks about more than healthy eating. God, let there be substance to him.

The next day, as my big date with Mike approaches, I go through my closet and dresser drawers to find something that compliments my shape. The red summer dress I got from Torrid and sandals will do. The dress makes my stomach look smaller, and the color brings out my skin undertones.

Why did he come to LA? Does he want a serious relationship, or does he have a BBW fetish?

After I'm dressed, I put a snack in my purse and then I'm out the door.

Mike offered to pick me up, but I insisted on driving myself because I don't know him well enough. Pulling up to the Bohemian restaurant near Pico and Hauser, I see Mike waiting for me, still looking ready for the gym in a T-shirt, black shorts, and Jordans. I glance at my red dress, wondering whether I'm overdressed. The restaurant didn't seem fancy when I looked it up on Yelp.

He spots me in my car and smiles and walks over as I rush to apply lip gloss. He opens my door, and I grin when he touches my arm.

"You found it," he says, smiling. "You're going to love this place."

As we enter the red brick building, Mike has to duck to avoid hitting the yellow and green umbrellas hanging from the ceiling. The Ethiopian waitress walks us to our seats. Mike seems out of place in his gym clothes, but I don't mind that. All around on the floor, customers sit on colorful Aladdin-style carpets, and every picture on the dark orange walls is of Black Jesus and his Twelve Apostles.

Dining on carpets is new to me, and this isn't a place I'd have chosen.

"How do you like it?" he asks when we get to our area.

"The ambiance is nice. Thanks for suggesting it," I lie. I'll never ask him to surprise me again. I exhale in relief as Mike successfully helps me on our purple and gold flying carpet, glad I didn't fall and embarrass myself.

"Have you exercised at Runyon Canyon?" Mike asks. "It's one of the most challenging outdoor workouts I've had since I've been here, but it makes me feel alive." Excitement dances in his eyes as he speaks.

"No, I haven't." What about me would make him think I enjoy a strenuous workout? Look at me. If it's difficult for him, how could I withstand it? Trainers have to stop prescribing the same workout to both obese people and thin people. "I wasn't expecting to eat on the floor," I say out of nowhere, desperate to change subjects because there has to be more to him. He's been spouting nonstop health crap since we've met.

"It's strange dining here at first," he admits, "but you'll get used to it." He smiles and rests his hand on my exposed shoulder. "You look gorgeous in that dress."

I smile back and do my best to ignore the surge of nerves that just tried to overtake me. "What brings you to LA?"

He shrugs. "There was nothing back at home for me. I came out here because I visited years ago and loved the weather. I saw several ads online for personal trainers. I did a phone interview and they hired me."

I twist my hair around a finger. "You're adventurous. I could do nothing like that."

He smiles and nods. "I put everything I could fit inside of the car and don't plan on looking back. People out here are more focused on working out and eating well. It's where I need to be."

I hold back a sigh. I knew he'd shift the subject back to working out.

"How many days a week do you work out?" he asks, squinting his eyes as if he knows I won't tell the truth.

This time I do sigh. Not again. Is he a diet detective? Maybe that's unfair of me to think, though. He *is* a personal trainer after all. What do I expect?

"On a good week, I walk for three days."

His face lights up. "You're lucky you met me. I'll show you how to take your routine to the next level."

The waitress brings the menu, and my eyes widen in shock when I see that the only options are lentils, impossible burgers, vegetables, and grains. This place isn't a meat-eater's paradise.

Mike looks deep into my eyes while slowly taking away the menu. "I'll order for both of us."

If he keeps looking at me like this, I'll eat whatever nasty food comes to our carpet. I can get a meal from Rally's afterward.

Desperate for a snack, I excuse myself to the restroom. Mike leaps to his feet to help me up, and I blush at how attentive he is. After ensuring the restroom is empty, I enter a stall and remove my snack from my purse. I can't trust Mike to fulfill my food needs, so I have to get creative. I take my time ripping the plastic package in case someone enters. I stuff my mouth full of butter toffee almonds, afterward brushing crumbs from my face and clothing and checking my teeth in the mirror for food before heading back to the carpet.

When he sees me walking back, Mike stands to help me down before jumping back into our conversation. I eventually learn that I enjoy his conversation when he talks about topics besides health. I shyly chuckle when he says, "I admire women who wear locs. I'd get some, but they'd get in the way when I'm working out."

I can't take my eyes off his athletic build. I want to melt staring at his blemish-free skin and the muscle grooves etched all over it.

As we wait for our food, he moves in closer, enveloping me with his woody and earthy scent. Letting his hand linger on my leg, he asks, "Do you know why I approached you that day?"

"I guess—" I start, but he interrupts.

"You're too pretty to be big. It's unhealthy," he says, his genuine expression unwavering. I can only stare back at him in shock and in rage.

"Too many black women are overweight," he continues, the sincerity in his voice only infuriates me more.

I shoot him a nasty look. "Who says something like that?" I ask. "Why did you invite me out if you have a problem with my size? Is everyone back East as rude as you are?" Hastily, I grab my purse. "Goodbye."

He stands, assisting me up. "I believe in speaking the truth," he says innocently. "Some men don't date bigger women, but I'm open-minded."

I give him a side-eye.

"Please let me explain," his mouth and eyes plead.

Still cautious, I ease back down as he gently squeezes my hand, not breaking eye contact. Whatever he has to say had better be good. I don't always think positively about myself, but that gives him *no right* to disrespect me.

"I'll put in work teaching you how to exercise and eat right. Free. I don't want to see you end up as another black woman with health problems." He caresses my leg with a look of bravado, like he's used to getting his way. "Do you have a health condition? You don't have to answer."

I shift uneasily, unsure how to read the situation.

"My mother died from diabetes three years ago," Mike confesses. "I should've done more to help her.

Nothing I can do about that now. That's why I want to help you."

"I'm sorry about your mother, but you shouldn't ask such personal questions. I'm not ill." I huff and fold my arms. "Are you attracted to me, or am I your charity? I don't need your help. CrossFit is down the street from me. If I needed a trainer, I would've signed up on my own." I pick up a vegan spring roll and bite it, surprised it tastes better than I would have imagined.

"I want to help. That's all," he insists. "Don't think of me as a trainer. I'm not charging you. How many trainers take clients out to eat?" He sips his cucumber and lime water. "Please don't be the woman who doesn't know a good man or a good offer when it's sitting across from her."

Has he lost his mind?

I should get out of here, but did he admit this is a date?

I could benefit from the situation by getting a boyfriend *and* losing weight.

I nod to myself, holding back a smile. Yes, I'll do this. If things don't work out, we'll go our separate ways.

"Maybe we can work something out. I'm open-minded." I reply eventually, still not fully trusting him.

The waitress brings our main course: veggie burgers, Brussels sprouts, and, for dessert, a fruit bowl. Mike digs into his burger while I nibble on mine. No wonder he stays so thin. Thank God I ate my snack in the restroom.

He later wipes vegan mayonnaise from his mouth and asks, "How do you like your food?"

"It's good," I mutter, not wanting to hurt his feelings. Being too nice is my problem.

After we finish our meal, he helps me up and then pays at the counter. Before parting ways, he gives me a lingering hug. "I had a good time. If you'll let me, I can cook for you. Think about it. I'll be in touch."

We pull away and I smile at him. "I do like a man who can cook," I admit. "Thanks for treating me. Goodnight."

Shortly after my date, I'm in my dining room smiling and giggling as I write what I ate for dinner in my journal. Today was a good day, and I'm anxious to see how my relationship with Mike develops.

CHAPTER 5

As I sit in the back row of OA, I watch as everyone claps as a blond leaves the podium, pushing up the bracelets slipping from her thin wrist. The facilitator soon after dismisses the group, and I'm relieved no one pressured me to participate. I'm content receiving the encouragement I need from listening to others. It feels good knowing I'm not the only one battling food obsession, however, I relate to the round people more than those who've identified as anorexic.

A woman with a salt and pepper pixie cut next to me stands to leave and swings a purse half her size onto her shoulder. Before she heads out, though, she extends her hand to me and we shake. "Nice to meet you," I nod to her and say.

"Keep coming to the group, young lady. We all need each other," the woman with the pixie cut says. "I've been an overeater for years. Coming here keeps me grounded. With God's help, we can succeed."

I say, "I'll definitely keep coming."

After rummaging through her purse, she hands me a book. I accept it, but I'm confused why she gave it to me. I glance at the title: *A Piece of Cake: A Memoir by Cupcake Brown.*

She taps the book in my hand. "This book showed me that change is possible for us all. It's based on a true story. I hope you'll read it and let it inspire you as it has me."

That's nice of her, but I haven't read a book since V. C. Andrews' *My Sweet Audrina.* I have some space in my closet for it.

"Thank you. Can't wait to read it," I lie. Then I stand and start to leave her. "I have to catch Ava before she goes," I say, waving to her as I go. After seeing her wave back, I make my way over to Ava.

Ava grins and stands to greet me. "You came back."

Her excitement is contagious, and I'm eager to share my progress. "I'm tracking my food, and I walked a few days last week," I say, pleased because it's the truth. "I'm proud of myself."

Her smile widens. "Awesome. Start sending me pictures of your meals because it will keep you honest about the amount of food you're eating. Call me if you get the urge to overeat so I can help you cope. The program works if you take full advantage of it."

"I'll get on top of it this week." She's asking a lot of me, but I'm positive I can do it.

"Last week, you opened up about your family," Ava says, her tone lowering so no one else can hear. "How were you feeling after? You seemed fine when we texted, but I want to make sure."

I shrug. "I was okay, and I'm doing good today. I'm still unsure how talking about the past will help," I say, not wanting her to pry too much today.

Ava nods understandingly. "I appreciate you for sharing your concerns. Last week, we identified some of your overeating triggers. You overeat when you experience intense emotions like anger and sadness. Stress management might help you curb those emotions, but we'll talk about that later. I'm glad your job isn't stressful." She pauses for a moment to rest her hand on mine. "Some of our sponsors have even quit stressful jobs to control their compulsive eating."

I think on her words for a moment. "That makes sense. It's not just intense emotions, though. It's hard to pinpoint why I overeat because I eat too much when calm or burdened." I hunch my shoulders, unsure how to explain to Ava what I don't even understand myself.

Noticing my hesitance, she touches my arm comfortingly.

"I can see why you'd be confused," she offers. "Food addiction is serious, and some chemical additives in food are highly addictive. Whatever the reason, following the 12 Steps and coming to the meetings will help."

"My reaction to food is a mystery to me. I'm still reviewing the literature. I'll ask if any questions arise."

"Call me anytime," she says. "I also wonder if relationships could be a major trigger seeing as you began overeating because of problems with your parental relationships. We could explore that another time if you're willing."

My eyes darken and I feel my fists clench at my sides. Mother and Aunt Pat both think they know better than me how I ought to live my life. Even the thought of them fills me with bitterness.

"Not a problem," I say, but I don't mean it.

Ava smiles. "Okay. Can we talk more about the early days of your eating struggles? I'll stop if it gets hard. When I opened up to my sponsor, I needed a box of tissues to continue. It's natural to have mixed emotions about the process."

I look over my shoulder to ensure no one is standing close enough to hear. "I think I can do that." I sigh, not knowing what questions to expect.

"Can you share more specifically how your eating habits changed after your mother left?"

I look down at my hands, which are tapping the book the pixie cut woman gave me. "Before she left, I was regular sized and ate regularly. She left, then I kept putting on weight." I turn in my seat, not knowing what more to say.

"You coped with her absence as best as you knew how. Some use alcohol, sex, drugs, and porn. We use food." She takes a drink from her container. "Were you dieting?"

My hands have left the book and are now interlocking and unlocking. "I was a professional dieter. My aunt Pat put me on every diet she was on: Jenny Craig, the cabbage diet, everything. Nothing worked, though, because I enjoyed fixing Thanksgiving-style feasts on Sunday mornings. The only thing I lost was the ability to see my neck." I laugh, but it fades when Ava doesn't join in. What's she thinking? Why didn't she laugh? That was funny. "Dad didn't notice my weight gain." Why did I say that about Dad? She'll probably follow up on that. Me and my big mouth.

"I'm surprised you didn't name the grapefruit diet. That was my go-to for weight loss." She chuckles, lost in a memory for a moment. "Why do you think your dad didn't notice?"

"He was depressed," I blurt out to defend him. "He did his best, and I won't take that away from him."

"I'm sure he did," Ava says with kind eyes. "Do you know where your mother is today?"

I laugh bitterly. "She came home my senior year. She had been living fifteen minutes away in Culver City the entire time. She and my dad got back together. We're not close."

Ava looks astonished. "You must have been mortified." She touches my shoulder. "How did they explain that?"

Her question is unsettling, and I'm tapping my foot. Mother's return is a sensitive subject to this day. I won't say much because I don't want to binge later from being pissed off. "They said she needed time to find herself." I look around because it's hard to look her in the eye when discussing how ridiculously my family handled that situation. I love my dad, but he could've given a better explanation.

Ava frowns, probably feeling annoyed too. "Anyone would've been angry. I recommend speaking to a psychologist to help with anger. There are referrals on the back table. I check in with my therapist periodically. What do you do for self-care?"

I sigh in relief at the change of subject. I can breathe again. "Listening to music brings me peace." I look at my new book. "A nice lady here gave me a book. I need to add more activities to my schedule, and I'll think about seeing a therapist," I say, wondering at what point she began assuming I could benefit from mental health services. My focus is on weight loss.

The room is clearing out, so I take the hint and stand to leave. Ava stands too and hugs me. "We'll talk later," she says. "Let's connect this week by phone and text."

Hours later, I sit on my sofa craving sweets. As a distraction, I reach for the book I got today at OA. The cover intrigues me because it's covered in rainbow sprinkles. Flipping it over, I read the back and discover Cupcake Brown, the author, went through hell and overcame it, and today she's a lawyer. I set down the book and read the Amazon reviews.

Whoa. She was on crack and experienced all types of hell.

If she can overcome tragedy, I know I can, too. I'm going to fight the urge to binge and pick up this book and get to reading.

As I'm turning a page, my phone sounds. It's a message from Mike, and I'm giddy reading it.

"Had a good time the other day. I'll call when I get off work. Do you work today?"

I waste no time replying.

"Had a good time too. Happy to hear from you. I'm off today and free."

"Want to go to the Hollywood Walk of Fame? I've not been since I got here."

I try to contain my elation, telling myself to play it cool and wait for a few minutes.

"Would love to show you around. Talk later."

The thought of seeing Mike again both excites me and fills me with questions. Does he have kids? Has he ever been married? My last name could be Shaena—

I pause because I don't know his last name.

The mysteries surrounding Mike make him so much more enchanting anyway. Having a personal trainer for a boyfriend and attending OA will make me slim in no time.

How did I get this lucky?

CHAPTER 6

My phone alarm awakes me early and I hit snooze. A second later, my cell sounds again, but this time it's a text from Ava. I sigh and roll over without texting back. I'm not ready to talk to her. It's been four months since I joined OA, and I'm conflicted on whether it's been helping me.

I've not lost as much weight as I would've liked. Five pounds isn't a huge accomplishment. It's gotten to a point where I occasionally don't attend the group. Everyone else shares, even people who started coming after me, while I just sit in the back and do nothing. I suspect they'll side-eye me if I don't open up soon. The members are friendly, but I'm not ready to divulge my secrets, not even to Ava.

She still doesn't know I binge. If I confess that, it'll be clear to everyone my life is out of control. On social media, some black women promote black girl magic and being a strong black woman, and I want those qualities. I don't see many strong women in my family and I want to change that. If I have kids, I want them to say I conquered whatever barrier came my way. But if I can't conquer my weight…

My mind drifts off into silence, not wanting to finish that thought.

My motivation for attending is learning from others. Stories of people overcoming longstanding food addictions makes me certain I, too, will succeed. Lately, I've been feeling motivated. I took Ava's advice of getting a hobby and took up making jewelry out of rubber bands, and the woman with the pixie cut always has kind words for me. I told her my name and, after I finished it, we chatted about the awesome book she gave me. If the author could become a lawyer after being in a gang and using crack, I can definitely meet my weight loss goals.

Groggy, I force myself to sit up in bed and read my text from Ava.

"I hope you're well. Haven't seen or heard from you in a week."

She's calling me out. What should I say?

"I'm good. I'll be back this week. I'm doing well with managing my eating."

"I'd encourage you to keep coming. Having a support group can keep you on track when life gets out of hand, and it always does. I look forward to seeing you."

After texting with Ava, I regret I wasn't truthful with her about my eating. It isn't the healthiest, but at least I cut down on binging to about twice a month. My life hasn't been hectic lately, so I don't need a psychologist's help. Nothing too stressful is happening at work, and I rarely see my parents to avoid Mother's criticism.

I get out of bed because Mike will be here soon. I wish he'd give me a title. I don't bring it up to avoid sounding pushy, but my parents don't even know he exists, and they won't until he claims me. They'd have questions I don't have answers to. Mike treats me like his client most of the time except for the occasional peck on the lips. He must like me, though, since he keeps coming around.

We've developed a morning routine. More accurately, he has made a habit of coming over in the morning, making me breakfast, and packing my lunch for work. His meals are nasty, but at least I get to spend time with him.

I'm roused from my thoughts by a knock at the door. Before answering, I grab the black and gold bracelets I made for Mike. I'm still getting the hang of making rubber band bracelets. It's something I liked as a child, and I find it relaxing.

I open the door to see he's carrying grocery bags. He bends over, pecks me on the lips, and heads for the kitchen. I roll my eyes. Maybe people from the East coast take things slow, but I want him to lay a big kiss on me.

I follow behind him. "I have something for you." I grin as I hand him the bracelets.

He accepts them and grins. "These are nice. You made them with my favorite colors." He puts them on and admires them. He pecks me on the lips again and sets down the groceries on the counter. Pulling out some fruit and white liquid, he heads for the blender. He catches me wrinkling my face as the concoction blends. "It's Kefir. It's great for digestion," he explains. "You'll love it." Mike smiles like that would be all it takes to convince me.

It looks horrible, but I reluctantly pour the smoothie into my container as he prepares my lunch. "You're going to love this tofu and spinach wrap."

I admire the muscles in his arms as he makes my wrap. "Thank you. I know it's delicious because you made it for me." He smiles broadly at my words, and I hug him.

"Got to go," he says. "See you after work."

I grab my smoothie and walk him out, tasting it on the way. It's tart, but not bad. He says he doesn't make dinner for me since he doesn't want to spoil me.

I chuckle as I relax onto the sofa after he leaves. Lucky me.

Stretching my legs out and covering up with a fuzzy blanket, I grab my journal on the living room table and add my breakfast.

After my morning shift, I sit in the break room with Monica and Carrie, two of my coworkers. I hand Monica two multicolor necklaces, one for her and one for her daughter, and I give Carrie blue and pink toe rings.

Carries seems touched by my gesture and removes her sandals to put on the toe rings. "These are cute. Thank you," Carrie says with a smile. "Where did you get these? I used to make these in art class back in the day."

I grin back. "I needed something to do when I'm bored. I bought the kit on Amazon, and I've been watching videos to learn how to make complicated pieces."

"That's awesome. I appreciate the jewelry. My baby will love them," Monica responds, standing. She then looks to Carrie. "It's time to pick up the food."

Carrie stands with her and looks down at me. "Girl, don't tell me you're not going to Kwon's with us."

I shake my head. "I brought lunch," I say, tapping my lunch bag on the table for emphasis.

"Good for you, Shaena," Monica says. "One day I'm going to bring lunch, just not today." She giggles as she puts on her shades and walks to the door with Carrie following behind.

You know what, I really don't want to eat Mike's food when I could enjoy scrumptious food with my friends, so why am I torturing myself?

"Wait for me," I call to them. I head to the garbage and empty Mike's lunch inside. "I'm ready." I toss my lunch bag back on the table and join the others.

"Why do you keep throwing that man's food away?" Carrie laughs as I fall in step with her. "Starving people would be mad." Carrie holds the front door and we walk to the stop light.

"That's wrong, Shaena," Monica adds, pushing the crosswalk button at the busy intersection. "Tell him you don't like his food so you can stop being wasteful." She lifts her hands in a gesture of innocence after I give her a look. "It's none of my business though."

"It's not that easy," I shoot back after we cross the street. "He's good to me, and I don't want to hurt his feelings. Next week, I'll eat his food." Carrie scrunches her face in disbelief as I hold the restaurant door for her.

As luck would have it, Mike texts while I'm in line to order food. I feel guilty about trashing his food and now standing in line to eat food not on his meal plan.

Carrie's leaning over looking at my screen. "Is that your boyfriend?" she asks.

I look up, frowning at her, and step out of line to view the text.

"How is the wrap?"

My fingers dart across the screen. "Couldn't be better," I type. "I appreciate all you do for me."

Seconds later, he responds. "No problem. Later."

When I get back in line, Carrie says, "I hope your man, who you haven't introduced us to, isn't texting your ungrateful self," Carrie says with one hand on her hip. "Wait until he finds out you're trashing his food."

Monica searches for change in her wallet. "The food isn't bad," says Monica. "Whatever type of rice dish you let me taste last week was good. It's not Kwon's, but it wasn't bad. I'll eat it next week if you change your mind."

After staring at them with a look of disbelief, I storm off without answering and take a fortune cookie from the counter.

They don't understand what I have to do to make this relationship work.

After collecting myself, I get back in line with the girls and pop half a fortune cookie into my mouth. "Everything will be okay. Trust me. No more throwing out yucky food. I'll introduce him when the time is right." I scrunch my face. "The three of us haven't hung out outside of work in months because we've all been busy."

"Excuses, excuses," teases Carrie, winking at a guy who just got in line.

"We could work out some time," suggests Monica. "I've had a lot on my plate lately, but I'll make time."

I nod. "We'll hang soon. I have to make time for you all." There's a chance I'm lying about getting together. I like them, but I've been too caught up with Mike lately. I'm not worried, though. It's normal to spend less time with friends when in a romantic relationship, and, besides, I see them five days a week at work anyway.

Once our food is ready, we walk back to work and eat. Since chicken fried rice isn't healthy, I skip that journal entry when I'm back at my desk. It's now my custom not to journal unhealthy food because I want to feel proud of my accomplishments when I look into my journal.

Later that evening, I'm on the couch reading a novel I bought from a thrift store when Mike calls me from the bathroom.

What does he want? Did I run out of tissue?

The door is open, and he's standing inside waving me in. Why is my measuring tape on the sink?

"I need to take your measurements." He steps toward me with the tape as if he knows I'll submit. "I need to weigh you, too."

"Why?" I ask, indignant at his audacity. "You make most of my meals. What, you don't trust me?"

He shouldn't trust me, all things considered, but this is weird.

"I want to track your progress." He rests a hand on my bathroom sink. "You'll be my first LA success story, and I have to make sure you lose weight."

I roll my eyes. "This is ridiculous and unnecessary. We never discussed my being your success story, so how did you make that decision?"

He huffs. "It's not a big deal, and I'm telling you now. I'd put your picture in my portfolio to brag about the work we did together. I'm helping you for free, I should get some benefit, don't you think?" His tone is conversational and easy, sounding as though he fully expects my compliance.

I cross my arms and grumble in frustration until I realize we both can benefit here. I help him with his work, and I get an extra accountability partner. The firm line of my mouth softens slightly. "If you think it'll help your business and help me lose weight, I'm in. You are helping me at no cost, and I appreciate you."

He grins as I walk toward him. He takes my measurement over my clothes and writes them in his notepad. Wrapping me in his arms, he kisses me intensely.

Is that his tongue? This a first.

What has gotten into him?

He lets go of me, and, shocked at his passion, I stare until he turns away. He slaps me on the butt and walks to the door. Going into full trainer mode must've turned him on. From now on, I'll put the scale and tape measure by the front door, so it's the first thing he sees. I now know what gets him going. That kiss removes all doubt about how he feels about me. He'll ask me to be his woman soon. I can feel it.

In the weeks that follow, we reach a really good place. I've been losing weight consistently thanks to him and OA, and I hardly even binge anymore. After the fuss Carrie and Monica made about Mike's food, I've been eating it. It's okay.

I'm actually not sure if my progress is from OA's tools or Mike, but I'm not complaining.

I continue to attend OA, but I'm still a silent observer. I've been learning more about coping skills and assertiveness training. I quit food tracking and stored my journal and the OA materials in my closet. Life is too short to write down every meal, and I'm doing well without it. I read the OA handouts several times, including the 12 Steps, and I might've memorized everything, so I don't need them. Truthfully, I can't follow the 12 Steps because I haven't admitted to anyone my true problem, so that's why I tucked it away in the closet.

I'd feel better if I was more committed to the program for Ava's sake because I value our relationship, but I'm not. She continues to call and text even when I'm inconsistent. She remains the only person to know I attend OA.

Mike and I are now hand in hand going into the mall to buy gym shoes. He has on my bracelets, and I'm wearing toe rings the same color of his bracelets. Mike swings my arm. "Let's go to the movies after we leave the mall," he says. "Are you up for that?"

Although we haven't had sex, I'm happy he's more affectionate, especially at weigh-ins. I really like him and want him to meet the people who are important to me, but not until he claims me as his woman. I have no suspicions he's seeing someone else, but if he wants me, he needs to say it. I don't want anyone else, so I hope we're on the same page.

I look up at him. "That sounds good. You pick the movie since I chose the last time."

As we're walking to the shoe store, there is a curvaceous woman walking toward us, licking her lips as she looks Mike up and down.

What's wrong with her?

She's rubbing her fingers through her long wig. It could be a weave, but that's not important. She looks at me and scowls when our eyes meet. I hold Mike's hand tighter and look up at him to make sure he's not checking her out because I'm jealous. She's gorgeous, and her body is my dream body. Mike was looking straight forward, but now looks down at me and smiles because I'm squeezing his hand.

The woman is closer now, and Mike stops abruptly to give me the sloppiest kiss ever in front of Macy's. People walk around us and stare, and a man covers a little boy's eyes. Though I'm self-conscious, the kiss is good, so I close my eyes, wanting this moment to last.

I open them a moment later, and that woman is gone. To the right of us, a group of teen girls are cheering us on and recording us. Mike laughs and points at the girls. "You see it," he says as the girls cheer louder.

His focus is back on me. "I'm hungry. You want dinner, too, after we leave?"

"I'd love that." Since I learned months ago not to let him choose the restaurant, he doesn't complain about where I decide to eat. I've found plenty of vegan and vegetarian restaurants around town to satisfy us both. I didn't know before that LA had so many selections.

After grinning up at him again, we head inside the shoe store. I couldn't be happier with my man.

CHAPTER 7

I'm pacing in my bathroom weeks later because my happy relationship is likely going to be over as soon as Mike gets back from his car. All the public affection will be done for if the scale isn't my friend today.

Today is weigh-in day, and I suspect I've put on pounds because I fell back into my old eating patterns. Ava warned me that would happen.

Recently, I've been trashing Mike's meals. I don't toss them at home in case he sees them in the trash. I lied and told Carrie and Monica he stopped cooking for me because of his schedule. I've been indulging in Chinese food and vending machine snacks instead, and more than I care to admit.

How can I eat healthy when my friends don't? Am I supposed to have a zucchini wrap while they eat egg rolls? Give me the latter any day.

I tap my feet against the cold tiles. He's still not back. I sit on the toilet lid biting my nails. He still hasn't given me a title, but I'm past that since there's no longer a need for one. Only insecure people need relationships defined, and this revelation is thanks to a male YouTube dating guru. He claims if women listen to him, they'll be married in no time. His tips helped me relax and appreciate that Mike wants to take things slow.

However, lately, I've wondered if Mike is religious. He doesn't go to church or talk about his beliefs, yet, I've never dated a man who didn't try to have sex with me. When we first met, he told me to be blessed. If he's religious, I wish he'd say so. There's no judgment here. Maybe he's celibate, but I don't want to ask and offend him. What if he leaves me? When the time is right, we'll take our relationship to the next level.

I look anxiously out of my bathroom door. What's taking him so long to find his notebook? I could take a laxative now, but it won't help with this weigh-in. If I attended OA regularly and participated, I wouldn't be in this predicament. I'm hanging on because hearing the members' journeys encourages me. Sometimes, I get a laugh when people talk about the things they've done to hide their eating disorders. One day, I'll get the guts to stand before the group and tell my story, but I'm waiting for the right moment. The perfect time will be when I no longer feel anxious about sharing.

The front door opens, then shuts. Mike shouts, "I'm going to the kitchen. Be right there."

He can take all the time he needs. I could tell him I don't want to be measured, but I don't want to upset him.

My phone sounds and it's Ava.

"Hope to see you this week. Consider reviewing your OA pamphlets on the days you don't attend. There's some good stuff inside. Miss you."

My fingers drum the back of my phone idly as I think of a response.

"Will do. Work has been hectic. I've not been eating healthy at all. I'm coming to a meeting on Sunday. Thanks for always checking in on me."

A moment later, another text comes in.

"Coming to the meetings will give you the strength needed to not overeat when stressed. Let me know if you need anything."

I hate lying to her about work, but I can't say I'm not attending because I don't always feel up to it. I want to enjoy my weekends lounging in bed on occasions. Other times, I do want to be there, but I'm self-conscious. What if members gossip about me because I come and don't get involved? It surprises me that she continues to suggest additional meetings considering my inconsistency. I'm not addicted to drugs or anything, so a few meetings a month is enough for me.

Mike finally walks into the bathroom with his notepad and wastes no time. "Are you ready?" he asks with an eyebrow raised.

Is he on to me? Do I look like I've gained weight?

I sigh, take off my shoes, and step on the scale and it reads two hundred and eighty pounds. My heart skips a beat when I see the number.

"What happened?" He looks at me like I'm a disappointment. "Are you cheating on your diet?" He shakes his head in disgust. "You gained two pounds."

"I don't know what happened," I lower my head and lie. "My period will be here any day. That could explain it. I've been doing everything you suggested."

"Tell the truth." He rests against the wall, writing in his notebook, not looking at me. "I can't handle being lied to."

I slowly step off the scale in shame and rub his shoulder. "I'm telling the truth."

He steps back and frowns down at me. "I'm disappointed you'd stand here and lie," he admonishes. "I gave you an opportunity to be real with me, but you couldn't even do that. You don't appreciate the things I do for you." He closes his notepad with a snap. "You're selfish and want everyone to do the work for you, but sadly, that isn't how life works."

I scoff. "Wow. I'm surprised to hear that's how you feel." I shake my head because I don't care for his accusations. "I always say thank you and I appreciate you. If you look into that notebook of yours, you'll see the work I've done." I purse my lips. "The numbers don't lie."

He mumbles something under his breath and walks out of the restroom. I follow him through my bedroom to the living room. "I didn't lie to you," I insist.

He opens the door, glares at me for a moment, and slams it.

Now I'm mad that he's angry. Stuff like this makes me want to eat. After glancing at my jewelry-making kit on the shelf in my living room, I collect it and walk to my closet where I store it next to other things I started and stopped, like my boxing attire and make-up kits. It's been a few weeks since I made jewelry anyway. The last things I made were bracelets and rings for Monica's daughter after Monica said she'd asked for more. I've lost my passion for it. One day I'll find something that holds my attention.

I put on my shoes and head off to the donut shop, feeling miserable about Mike and the weight gain.

This day sucks. Since I've already gained the weight, might as well buy sweets.

My alarm blares to wake me the next morning, forcing me to roll awake and get ready for work. Mike still hasn't texted me back since our blowup yesterday.

I hope he doesn't hold what happened against me. I lied only because I felt guilty. He wouldn't understand if I told him food calls me and I go running towards it. Take last night for instance; I had four donuts because I was stressed, sad, and angry with myself and with Mike. Eating junk food to cope wasn't my proudest moment, but I don't count it as a binge.

I don't want to be this way. It's not my fault.

I'm dressed, and he should be here in a minute. I'm sticking to my period weight gain no matter what happens. A gain sucks, but it's only two lousy pounds. Come on. Not that big of a deal.

I look at the time on my phone and he's late.

This isn't like him.

When it's obvious he isn't coming, I head to the kitchen to make my own breakfast.

Does his absence mean he hasn't forgiven me?

He needs space, so I won't bother him today.

Although I stopped eating his meals, I've gotten used to our routine, so I try to make the smoothie myself. Unfortunately, I put too much fruit and not enough liquid in the blender, and now the blender is stalling. I add more liquid and taste it. Not as good as Mike's, but I pour it in my container anyway. I later leave for work, uncertain of my relationship status.

Later that afternoon, I'm walking into the break room with Monica and Carrie with Kwon's take-out in my hand. We sit and are about to dig in when Mike texts. If he's breaking up with me, I shouldn't prolong it. He said some mean things to me yesterday. I don't want us to end, but I can't force him to stay.

"What's for lunch?"

The brevity of his text isn't lost on me, and I type out the first lie that comes to me.

"Hey, you. Barley salad. Are we good?"

A moment later, Mike replies.

"Liar. I saw you and two women coming from a Chinese spot. You were carrying a to-go bag."

His accusation startles me, and I pause for a moment before answering.

"Are you stalking me?"

"Don't go to that place because you could get tempted. Do you want to die like my mother?"

"The food was for my supervisor. Why are you bringing your mother into this? And why are you following me? That's not okay and it's weird."

A moment later, he texts.

"I've worked too hard for you to eat crap food."

"It wasn't for me. Answer me. How do you know where I was?"

He wastes no time following up.

"I'm in the area. Do you seriously think I'm stalking you? Everything isn't about you. Prove you're telling the truth by coming to the gym later."

I frown.

"I don't know how coming to the gym proves I'm not a liar. I know everything isn't about me, and I'm far from self-centered. It's strange that you saw me and didn't speak, but I'll see you at the gym and we can talk more."

A few minutes pass, and he doesn't reply, so I put my phone away and joke and eat with Carrie and Monica.

Carrie runs her fingers through her curly pink wig. "How do you all like my new wig? Don't lie."

Monica and I look at one another and cover our mouths, giggling." It looks like something you'd wear," I say through my fingers.

The break room door suddenly flies open, and Mike rushes to our table, glaring eyes on me. "Put down the egg roll," he demands.

My mouth drops, and the beef-filled appetizer tumbles to the floor just as I was about to dip it in some sweet and sour sauce.

I know he doesn't mean to humiliate me at my job, but I've never seen him this angry. His body is stiff, his nostrils are flared, I think I see fire behind his eyes, and his breathing is shallow. It's scary.

Why would he do this? How did he get past security?

At least it's only my friends and me here. I have to get him to leave quickly to minimize this situation later with my friends.

I slowly stand, signaling to the door. "Let's talk outside." I want to stay calm, but he's looking at me like I've done something extremely wrong. I'm fuming, but I have to keep it together in front of my friends.

"Is everything good?" asks Carrie, putting down her fork. "Who is he? Is that your guy?"

"Don't worry," I say, manifesting a calmness I don't feel. "It's a misunderstanding. That's Mike."

Inside, I know everything is not okay. Mike is here acting crazy.

"That food isn't on your diet plan," he accuses, pointing at my meal and ignoring the glares of my friends and my exasperated expression. "Shaena, have you been lying after everything I've done for you? I asked if you were eating at that—"

"Please leave. We'll talk later," I interrupt. Who does he think he is? What have I done to make him think he can treat me like this? "This is my job. Are you trying to get me fired?" I signal again for the door, but he ignores me.

"Should we call security?" Monica asks me before turning to Mike. "You should leave," she scolds. "Stop causing a scene. This is a corporate office."

"She's safe with me," he says dismissively. "This has nothing to do with you two." He turns his attention back to me. "See what you've done? You have these people thinking something is wrong with me when you're the problem."

Carrie and Monica exchange a look of disbelief, fixing their hard eyes on Mike. Trying to stay professional, I say as calmly as I can, "*Go*. I'll talk to you later." I put my hands together, pleading for him to go. "Get out of here before my supervisor comes. Stop it."

He doesn't move. I try to grab his arm, but he quickly pulls away. My friends move closer to one another and whisper. I want to disappear. What are they saying about me?

"Let me go," Mike grunts, yanking away from me. "Your only concern should be why you thought it was okay to lie."

I let him go, wishing he'd leave on his own. "If you weren't spying on me, this wouldn't be happening. Everyone deserves a cheat day. I would *never* come to your job and behave like this."

"You're like a drug addict. Food is your weakness." He paces next to me. "Would you tell a recovering alcoholic to indulge in a cheat day?"

"We're going for help," says Monica as she and Carrie walk to the door.

"*No!*" I scream, immediately regret raising my voice. What he's doing is wrong, but I don't want him to go to jail. He could get a record or be killed by the police. The security guard would probably throw him out, but then staff and management would know Mike is here because of me. I could be written up or thought of as unprofessional. "He's leaving. Don't get anyone else involved," I say in as calm of a tone I can manage.

They look at me and then at one another like they don't believe me, but they slowly move back to their seats.

"Mike, it's not fair to compare me to a drug addict." I walk closer to the door, wanting him to follow, but he doesn't. Why is he so stubborn? He can't be reasoned with. "We need privacy. Walk with me, *please*."

Monica's and Carrie's mouths are open while they watch from the edge of their chairs.

"She's a good person," Carrie asserts. "I don't know what's wrong with you, but you're wrong for this."

Mike glares at her, probably about to go off, but I come to her rescue. It's one thing for him to disrespect me, but I won't have him doing it to my friends. "Get out of here, you food Nazi! You're only happy when I'm losing weight. Are you my dad, trainer, or my boyfriend?" I'm on a roll but feel dumb because my friends now know how dysfunctional I am, and their expressions of horror only make me feel worse. Outbursts like this are why I can't speak at OA. My flaws always have a way of seeping out. "Do you treat all your girlfriends like this? You knew I liked to eat when you met me. Either love me for me or dump me."

He's never admitted to loving me, what am I saying?

He snatches my Styrofoam box and storms to the garbage can a few feet away. "What are you doing?" I fume, enraged now. "I paid for that. You had better not—"

Disregarding the rage in my voice and the gasps of my friends, he lingers over the garbage can, holding my food above it.

"I know he's not about to do what I think he's about to do," Monica says.

A tense moment later, he slams the food container in the trash. Afterward, he rubs his hands together like he got a disease from touching it and is trying to get it off. I run to him and pull his arm, attempting to shove him out the door, but my efforts are in vain. He's too strong. "Who in the *hell* do you think you are? Sick bastard!"

"You need to go, *now*," Monica shouts, running toward Mike and me. "Stop disrespecting my friend." Monica is at my side, leaning in his face as she shouts. "Forget this, I'm getting security." She spins away from us and pushes open the door.

"No!" I yell after her. "Don't involve security. I got this under control," I lie again. I can't find the truth within me.

Puzzled, she stops to look at me in amazement as Mike yells at her. "Mind your business. I'm doing this because I care." Carrie moves to Monica's side as Mike launches into a frenzy, veins bulging in his neck and face. "You weren't concerned, or you would've stopped her from eating that mess."

"*Don't* talk to my friends like that," I reprimand Mike fiercely. "What part of leave don't you understand?" I keep pushing, but he remains fixed in the same spot.

"If you don't go now, security will come back here. You don't want to go to jail. Do you?" warns Carrie.

He ignores Carrie and glances down at my arms as I push him. "I've not been physical with you. Let me go," he commands. "It's either me or the MSG. I'm not wasting my time and skills with someone addicted to high fructose corn syrup. Were you ever eating the food I made for you?"

I stop pushing and stare without saying a word. I don't owe him an answer after the way he treated me.

"So, you're not going to say anything?" he shouts.

I stare back, still silent.

At last, after a heated moment of staring and glaring, he storms out of the break room.

I'm shaking with anger. No one has *ever* treated me like he has in public. Monica puts her arm around me and leads me to the table. I rest my head in my hands, wishing I'm invisible. I don't want to explain what happened, but I don't have a choice.

Why would he barge into my job, of all places?

After I calm my breathing and my nerves, my friends confront me. "Girl, why are you with someone like that?" Carrie leans toward me, eating her rice. "Has he ever done that before? Is he hitting you?"

"I don't know what got into him. He's never done anything like that," I say before looking up from my hands. "And no, he's never hit me."

How can Carrie eat at a time like this?

"What red flags did you miss? There had to be some. No one becomes that way overnight," Monica states. "Is he mentally ill, on drugs, or worse? You can do better." She wants to hug me; I can see it in her eyes.

"He's not on drugs." I sigh, disliking the question. I'm a private person. Until today, the only thing they knew about my relationship is that we were happy and that we worked out together. "He's fanatical about weight loss. That's all."

"Are you taking up for him?" Carrie is staring at me with her head cocked to the side. "You had better dump him."

Before I answer, Monica interjects, "You deserve better and shouldn't put up with verbal abuse. Be grateful management didn't walk in. Love you, but you need to set boundaries."

I sniffle. "I hear you both, and you don't have to worry about that happening again. I'm not stupid. I'm not taking up for him."

"I'm going to put it out there since I know Monica won't," says Carrie, putting her hands on her hips. "Why didn't you tell us Mike is so *handsome*?" She sighs and fans herself with her hands, giggling. "No wonder you've been hiding him."

Talking about him is the last thing I want to do. I give her a look that brings her grins to a halt.

Monica shakes her head. "Now is not the time. He has a mean spirit, and that makes him ugly."

Carrie's eyes turn downwards as she sips her iced tea.

Common sense should've told her it was bad timing. That's my girl, but I'm in no mood to play. She probably was trying to lighten the mood, but it's going to take a minute before I shake off what happened.

Six months of my life wasted.

The only good thing about today is my girls having my back; I appreciate their friendship. Had I opened up to them about my relationship, they could've warned me. Being secretive isn't always good.

Lunch time is over, so we leave the break room and I return to my desk.

Back at my cubicle, I pretend to work because I'm too overwhelmed to do anything more. It's hard to think of anything besides what happened at lunch. I know I can count on my friends to keep my secret because we've been working together for twelve years, but I can only imagine what would've happened if there were other staff members in the break room. Office gossip is normally scandalous, but how would they talk about what happened between Mike and me?

I imagine the gossip would go something like this: "Can you believe her boyfriend yelled at her for eating Chinese food and threw it in the trash? You know, that wouldn't be me putting up with that. Kwon's isn't cheap anymore. And the strangest part is her boyfriend gave her an ultimatum: vegetable grease or him."

CHAPTER 8

I'm on the sofa after work reflecting on the chaotic day I just had, too keyed up to watch TV, read, or listen to music. I've been debating on whether to call Mike for hours. He needs to explain himself because what he did was *not* okay. He claims he was in the area, but the whole thing was weird. Why not say he was outside when he texted? And what made him come into my office?

My phone suddenly chimes. I pick it up and it's a message from Monica.

"I'm checking on you to make sure you're okay. He was awful for doing what he did. Don't let him talk his way back into your life. Call me if you want to talk. Have a great weekend."

I smile a little as I type out a response.

"I appreciate you for checking on me. Today was a lot to deal with, and I'm sorry you had to witness it. Talk soon."

"You have nothing to apologize for. Sleep well."

The smile spreads knowing that Monica supports me. I text Carrie to see how she's doing after the blow-up, and then I call Mike because he is *not* getting away with what he did. He picks up on the first ring.

I don't waste time getting to the point. "What you did was unacceptable. Who comes to someone's job and makes a scene? How did you think I'd react?" I'm on the couch waving my empty hand furiously in the air. "I had a cheat day, and you judged me. How would you like it if I embarrassed you on the job?"

It was more than a single cheat day, but he doesn't need to know. He should feel bad for how he treated me since I didn't deserve that.

I'm shocked he hasn't tried to cut me off once. He waits a moment before he takes a deep breath and responds. "I'm sorry you're upset, but you're to blame for everything that happened. I gave you plenty of chances to come clean." His voice is calmer than I imagined. It's as though I'm emotional and he's rational. "Depending on the decision you make about your eating habits, you may never see me again."

"Are you freaking kidding me?" I'm yelling so loud that the neighbors might hear. "Now you're threatening to break up with me? You need to apologize, jerk."

Silence.

He hung up.

Now I'm livid.

How can he be so cruel?

Late that evening, as I toss and turn in bed, I'm burning in irritation. I can't stop thinking about how Mike humiliated me *and* hung up on me. All his actions today show he has zero respect for me. He can take his diet and shove it.

I had hoped to hear from Carrie, but she hasn't replied to my text yet. I can't stop thinking about food. I sing to myself and stare at the wall as a distraction, but it's to no avail. My mind is screaming that it wants sweets and fried food. I keep telling it no, but the pleas for fattening and sweets gets so loud that anxiety consumes me and I can't stop turning in bed. I can't get out of my mind "Voodoo Doll" by Fergie.

Is my problem with food like that of an addict? I imagine it is.

There's only one thing that'll stop this torture.

I get out of bed hungry and pull on my clothes. I then grab my purse and keys and head out to the car. I'm driving to the nearest Wingstop when all of a sudden Mike calls and keeps calling when I don't answer. I let him go to voicemail. When I finally get there, I park and go inside to get some food. I should call Ava, but I deserve good food after what happened today.

I'm standing in line to order, the smell of the food filling my head as I wait. It smells greasy. Twenty wings are all I'll buy. When it's my turn to order, I tell the woman to please give me forty deep-fried, lemon-peppered, boneless wings.

I know myself, and twenty won't satisfy me. My quick thinking will save time and gas. If only I show as much concern for my body as I do for my gas tank.

As I wait for my order outside of Wingstop, I pace back and forth. This cheat meal will be the last time I have greasy food, so I'd better cherish it. Tomorrow, I'll resume my diet. When my name is finally called, I grab my food and leave.

Before heading home, I go to Vons Grocery Store. I have to go. After all, what's a binge without sweets? I head to the bakery and examine all the beautiful cakes of various sizes and colors. In my hands ends up a vanilla cake with whipped cream frosting, multi-color flowers, and a blue happy birthday sprawled across it.

No one is nearby. I hold the cake and bend down, placing my nose on the plastic container. It smells of sugary bliss. I can feel my mouth salivating. Once I put it in my cart, I find myself staring at a chocolate cake layered with chocolate icing. Nah, I eventually decide that's too much chocolate.

If people weren't around, I'd open the plastic container and dig into the vanilla cake right now. The sugar and fat are calling me.

I hold myself together and walk a few feet to the cookies. Do I want cake or cookies? I've got to choose wisely, as whatever I get will be the last dessert I ever have. I grab a clear package of what I think are soft chocolate chip walnut cookies, but they look hard up close, so I put them down.

The ice cream is ahead. I inspect a single serving of Ben & Jerry's Cherry Garcia Ice Cream but then toss it back, instead opting for the pint.

When I pig out, I do it big.

Walking to the line, I'm ashamed. I get in line with only one woman ahead of me, and I wait until she walks off before putting my items on the conveyor belt. She was thin, and I didn't want her judging me. What would people think if they glanced inside my cart? Can they sense I'm having a pity party all on my own, or will they think I'm having a get-together? Let it be the latter.

My cashier, whose neck is covered in multicolored tattoos, is looking at me, probably wondering why I took so long to load my food.

Why didn't I order from InstaCart? That's what I'll do next time.

Wait, what am I talking about? Next time? I'm going to stick to a healthy lifestyle after this binge.

To my dismay, the cashier bags my groceries slowly. People are now in line behind me. I can feel their judgmental eyes on me. I focus on the cashier as she charges me ten cents for a plastic bag. "Are you having a party?" she asks, still packing my stuff. "Vons bakery makes the best cakes."

"My nephew's birthday is tomorrow. He loves the cakes here," I fib. Why couldn't she just do her job and leave me alone? I come in here all the time and no cashier ever holds a conversation with me.

Just my luck.

"How old is he?" she asks, ignoring the man behind me that's mumbling his frustration about our conversation.

I disregard him because I'm not confrontational, and engaging with him will prolong feasting. "He's seven." I don't like to lie, but she forced me. Why does she have to be so friendly?

She says, "Wish him a happy birthday for me."

I grin, quickly grab my things, and leave. I'm jittery with anticipation for my food splurge. In my hands are my favorite desserts, and I couldn't be happier. Few things bring this big of smile to my face the way food does.

When I get back in the car, I text and call Mike, but I get no answer. He needs to apologize for everything and explain why he was stalking me. Should I file a police report? I won't know until I talk to him. I contemplate going to his house to confront him, but my food calls for my attention, so I head home.

Because there are no cars around me, I lean over and take a fork from the glove compartment and dig into the cake on the side of me. I inhale it. Whipped cream is all on my hand, but I don't care. I lick it off.

My self-control is gone. I can't stop eating.

I'm on a diet once this is over. No need for guilt.

I exhale. That thought makes me feel better.

When I later pull up to my apartment, Mike still hasn't called back. I check my face in the rearview mirror to ensure no evidence of whipped cream remains. Next, I scan my surroundings, because it's too late for anyone to be outside, especially a single woman. Exiting the car, I quickly collect my things to avoid the neighbors. They know I'm single and might wonder why I have a birthday cake. I could explain Wingstop, but not the cake. Would they be able to see I'd already eaten some of the cake? Maybe they'd think I had left-over dessert from a party.

Not wanting to make two trips to the car, I balance everything in my arms and pray nothing drops. Successfully, I get through the main entrance and step into the courtyard. No one here. With a deep exhale, I focus on the door and make my way up the stairs. My arms burn from carrying all the food, but I finally, I reach the door and turn the knob, my heart racing.

I'm about to tear this food up.

I throw my keys on the end table and lick my lips as I set the food on the kitchen table. Should I text Ava?

I don't have to follow through on this binge, but I've come too far to turn back now.

I change into jogging pants with an elastic waist and head back to the kitchen. I would use a smaller plate to show restraint, but who am I kidding? Forty wings wouldn't fit on that. I cut the mangled cake, lick the sweet cream from the knife, and put a large chunk in a bowl topped with ice cream. I carry it all to the living room and turn on Netflix before sitting on the couch. It doesn't take long for me to eat ten wings, and it's all Mike's fault. I pause from eating to make Mike feel guilty because he needs to see what I did after he embarrassed me. I text him pictures of me in my sweatpants, lying across my sofa eating chicken wings, and then another with me licking whipped cream from my finger. It's not my best moment, but I'm angry. Why'd he treat me like I was lower than nothing?

He finally texts back when I'm half-done eating, but I refuse to read his replies. I've eaten so much my stomach hurts, but I keep going, refusing to be wasteful.

This dessert isn't too sweet, and it's deliciously moist. They must've added extra eggs and vanilla pudding. One part of me says to stop stuffing myself, but the gluttonous part won't listen. It tells me to worry about dieting tomorrow. YOLO.

Each bite of sweets sends me to a peaceful place where I zone out until my stomach won't allow more food. It's obvious I made a bad decision.

Is it too late to call Ava?

I won't call. I did this to myself, and now I'm dealing with the consequences.

I get in bed, bloated, never replying to Mike.

The next morning, I wake with a pounding head that's echoed by an incessant beating at my door. I reach for my phone to see that it's just after seven in the morning. I turn back over because I'm too full to move.

A wave of guilt suddenly hits me. I should've reached out to Ava, but I fought the urge to binge for as long as I could.

To my dissatisfaction, the knocking persists. I reluctantly kick my blankets to the ground, walk to the door, and look through my peephole. "I know you're in there," Mike says on the other side of the door. "Open up and stop playing."

I frown. "Go away. I don't feel good. You can text me why you did what you did. Do I need a police report for stalking?"

A neighbor approaches Mike and asks if he needs help. "Mind your business," he mutters in response.

From the sound of retreating footsteps, I can only assume my neighbor walked off. Mike could've gotten me fired, and now he's jeopardizing my housing. Is he trying to make me homeless? Does he hate me that much?

"I'm concerned about you. You need help, Shaena," says Mike through the door. "After what I told you about my mother, you sent me those pictures, and now you're ignoring me. Remember the ultimatum. Open the door so I can make your favorite smoothie. We can start over."

His concern softens me because really I do need help. I want to let him in because I could use a friend. Carrie still hasn't gotten back to me, and I don't want to bother Monica since it's early. If I let him in, I'll have to be clear that we're over.

Wrestling with indecision, I watch him pace back and forth in front of my door. I want that apology, and I might get it if I am real with him. I don't want to tell him how bad off I am, but I suspect he knows because I sent those pictures. Minimizing yesterday's binge is the answer. I'll tell him that it only happens after extreme stress.

Who better to help me than a trainer and a self-taught nutritionist? Surely he knows people like me. I won't tell him about OA because then he'll really think I'm out of control. He probably has a special meal plan and supplements for me. Am I deficient in vitamins?

I'm so desperate for a friend that I'll take Mike. It's too early to call Ava, but I'll see her tomorrow.

Despite my anger, I open the door. Walking into the living room, he closes the door and stands in front of me, looking me up and down. I look down to see there's grease and whipped cream on my pajama shirt. He sighs and heads to the kitchen, me walking behind him. "Why are you walking through my apartment? We have to talk about yesterday, and I have something to tell you. Come to the living room," I say, thinking he doesn't understand we're no longer an item and his days of walking through my place are over.

From behind him I notice him looking at the empty containers strewn across the counter. He turns around. "What in the hell is going on here?" he demands.

I'm speechless. My home was never a mess when he was around, but a good enough boyfriend, or ex-boyfriend, would make an exception for me this once.

"You have nothing to say?" He glares down at me. "You take one step forward and two steps back. Get help." He stares me up and down again, making me feel worthless. "You could've told me you were a binge eater. Are you bulimic? Do you make yourself vomit, too? I saw laxatives in the bathroom before. Now it all makes sense."

"Stop it," I say. "You're being toxic. Leave. Now. Don't ever talk to me like that again. Don't ever come here again."

Instead of leaving, he shakes his head. "You could've confided in me, and I would've helped. Because of your lies, my time has been wasted," he says, jabbing a thumb at his chest.

I'm lost for what to say or do to get him out of my apartment.

This wasn't what I needed from him. I should've woken Ava.

"You'll realize you had a good man one day," he goes on. "I was spending time with you when I could have been with clients who don't lie." His wide eyes on me are telling me I've ruined his life.

Finally, words come to me, and I'm passionate. "What happened to the loving Mike who stood on the opposite side of that door? You, as a personal trainer, should know that dieting is a process." I lean in and holler. "I'm not bulimic. I binged last night, and it's all your fault. Not everyone is as dedicated as you. Are you like this with your clients?" I throw my hand toward the front door. "Go. I'm better than this. I'm better than you. You're nothing but a selfish control freak."

"We're done," he says, frowning as he walks around me. "You made your decision. Liar. Lose my number." With that, he storms out of the apartment, slamming the door behind him.

I go back to bed with regret for sending the pictures and for letting him inside my apartment. I'm not the only one disgusted with myself now; Mike finds me re-pulsive, too.

I'm conflicted. A part of me cares what he thinks about my binging, and the other part hopes he suffers for all he's done. He does have some nerve, I'll give that to him, but my dad didn't raise no fool. I deserve better.

Mike's the one who wasted my time. It was six months, and I had no title. We only really talked about fitness, and he never made a move to have sex and never explained why. Obviously, he wasn't into me as much as I was him. How stupid was I to let him into my apartment after what he did to me? If my neighbor tells the landlord what Mike said to him in the hall, I can expect a call from the landlord.

At least we're through.

A phone alert sounds. I shoot up and read it. It's from Mike.

"I'll forgive you if you apologize for all that you've done to me. I'm hurt by your lies, and you won't take accountability. I'll get you some help."

His insolence fills me with righteous indignation.

"Go to hell!!! We're done!!!"

I shove my phone harder than expected, and it falls to the floor where it stays for hours.

CHAPTER 9

My roomy flower print dress dances around my ankles as I cross the street to OA the next day. As soon as I reach the other side, I feel my phone buzz. I pull it out of my purse, hoping to hear from Carrie. Even Monica texted me again late last night. To my dismay, it's just spam telling me my car warranty has expired. I mark it as spam, delete it, and toss the phone back in my purse. My car warranty is just fine.

The walk hasn't been good because I keep thinking about all the binges I had this year. Yesterday's binge weighs heaviest on my mind. Why do I keep binging? I can't count the times I promised to never do it again.

This merry-go-round I'm on is no fun, and I want off. I don't want to be forty and in this same predicament, but that's where I'm headed if I don't change today. I've got to make better use of OA.

So far, I've been lazy by not applying myself in the group and wasting Ava's time. I had everything I needed to be successful and failed to make the most of it.

I've had it with being out of control. I'm dedicating myself to overcoming bulimia.

My footsteps falter, and I stumble on the sidewalk in front of OA. Did I just admit, even if only to myself, to having bulimia?

I'm not supposed to say that word. Claiming the disorder would mean there's something wrong with me.

Right?

Am I one of those sick people?

Am I damaged?

Nana said not to claim any problem, but maybe she was wrong. Nana died from hypertension despite not naming or claiming it.

I've tried her way for long enough.

I've denied bulimia for years, but it has a way of sneaking up on me each time I think I've beaten it. How bad would it be if I came to terms with it?

Could refusing to say the word bulimia be the reason I haven't had lasting results? It's time I reconsider my thinking.

Yes, I'm bulimic, but I believe I won't always be bulimic.

I can't lose hope.

A few minutes later, Ava walks up the sidewalk as I pace outside the doors. When she reaches me, she wraps her arms around me, no questions asked about my pacing. I fight back tears to avoid ruining her yellow wrap dress because it really compliments her dark skin and ruining it would be borderline sin.

"What's wrong?" she finally asks.

Through sniffles, I manage to get out, "I binged last night, and my ex-boyfriend, Mike, knows I have bulimia. I've dealt with bulimia for years, but was too ashamed to tell you. I've been lying to you, Mike, and to everyone. Please forgive me."

Whew. I finally told someone. She's not laughing, and I didn't die of shame when the words passed my lips.

"You're being honest now, and that's all that matters. The lies you've told yourself outweigh the ones you told others." When she releases me from her embrace, seeing her sincere expression tugs at more tears. "You don't owe me an apology."

I wipe at my nose. "I feel horrible for being dishonest."

"Do you know how many times I lied to myself and to my family about my eating disorder?" Ava says, looking me in the eyes. "You wouldn't want me as your sponsor if you knew. I was destroying lives all around me just to keep my secret. You're at the right place, and I'm glad you came." She places her hands on my shoulders. "You're not alone, even though it may feel that way." She points to the OA building. "Inside there is a group of people who've been where you are, and they can help guide you to a healthier life. That is, if you're ready to stay honest and get consistent."

It's hard to process what I'm hearing. I begin a small smile. I'm going to commit, and this is going better than I could have imagined.

"I'm proud of you for acknowledging to others you have an eating disorder," Ava says, gripping my shoulders. I hug her again, her vanilla scent soothing me. "OA works if you follow the program," she says, "Admit you're powerless over your disease and accept you need the help of your Higher Power to stop compulsive eating."

I nod, letting her go. "I'll do it today. It's time. I'm ready to do whatever it takes to get control over my life. I was terrified of opening up in the group because I don't like admitting I have problems, but I'm ready."

She waves, acknowledging other members waking toward the building, turning back to me when she's done. "You'll get stronger by participating. I speak from experience. Many of us were scared the first time.

We might seem like pros, but that's only because we have been sharing for years."

I wipe my watering eyes. "You've given me a lot to think about."

I take her hand as we walk to the door. I'm still uncertain how much the meetings will help since I've never applied myself, but I'm tired of feeling helpless to food.

What have I got to lose?

Usually, I'm reluctant to walk through those doors, but today, I don't even need so much as a nudge. I willingly step through the doors, and, for the first time since joining OA, I feel a sense of hope.

ACKNOWLEDGMENTS

I thank God for His inspiration. I'm thankful to everyone who helped with this project: the readers of the original novella, the cover designer, beta readers, and the editors.

ABOUT THE AUTHOR

Samyra Alexander was born and raised in Gary, IN, and lives in Southern California. After receiving a D in 4th grade Art, she was told she lacked creativity, but the yearning to express herself never faded. She turned to words, finding a creative spark that resulted in writing several novellas. She holds a Doctorate in Clinical Psychology and explores mental health issues and their accompanying social taboos within the context of creative fiction. Follow her on Facebook at Samyra Alexander Author Page and YouTube and Instagram using her handle @TellSamyra or email tellsamyra123@gmail.com

www.ingramcontent.com/pod-product-compliance
Lightning Source LLC
Chambersburg PA
CBHW031745150726
47989CB00006B/2602